GILLY GILHOOLEY

A TALE OF IRELAND

by Arnold Dobrin

Crown Publishers, Inc., New York

The text of this book is set in 14 pt. Kenntonian.
The illustrations are 3/color pre-separated ink and wash drawings
with wash overlays, reproduced in halftone.

Library of Congress Cataloging in Publication Data

Dobrin, Arnold.
    Gilly Gilhooley; a tale of Ireland.
      SUMMARY: After quitting two jobs in a temper,
Gilly learns to control it and still get what he wants.
    [1. Anger—Fiction]   I. Title
PZ7.D66Gi3   [E]   74-19337

To the Irish—in gratitude for laughter

When Gilly Gilhooley was old enough to go to work, his father said, "It is time you went into the world, my lad. You're a strong boy and a clever one too. But don't go losing your temper over every little thing. Remember the laughter that is in you."

Gilly kissed his mother and father good-bye and started down the road.

He had a quick temper it was true, but he did not have time to think about that now. He wanted to find a job as soon as possible.

At the first farm he came to, he asked, "Is there
any work here, sir?"

"There's work here all right—plenty of work
for a boy who'll work hard!" replied the farmer
gruffly. "Do you know what it means to work *hard?*"

"Oh, yes I do, sir," said Gilly. "Just give me
a chance!"

"The job is yours," said the farmer as he showed
Gilly to his cabin.

The next few days Gilly was busy planting.
He planted beans and he planted peas.

He planted lettuces and he planted carrots.

He worked so hard that one morning he
was ten minutes late going to the field.

"Be on time tomorrow!" scolded the farmer.

But Gilly Gilhooley didn't like being told what to do. "You can take your farm and go to the Devil," shouted Gilly, and he picked up his hat and walked away.

A few hours later Gilly came to another farm. It was bigger and richer than the first. The farmer was drinking his tea when Gilly knocked at the door.

"I'm looking for a job," said Gilly. "You can trust me to do a good day's work."

"Well now—let me see," said the farmer. "Do you like pigs?"

"Oh yes," said Gilly. "I like pigs very much."

"Hmmmmmm," said the farmer. "Can you milk a cow?"

"Milked cows ever since I was a little boy," said Gilly.

"Is that so?" said the farmer. "Can you ride a horse?"

"With a saddle and without!" said Gilly.

"Well," said the farmer as he sipped his tea, "you sound like a good worker. The job is yours."

Throughout the day   Gilly fed the pigs,

milked the cows,

and dug potatoes.

After supper the farmer took Gilly up to the hayloft.
"Here you are," the farmer said.

"This is where you will sleep. Nothing like hay to make a sweet-smelling bed."

"Then *you* sleep in it!" snapped Gilly. "When *I* sleep, I sleep in a real bed!"

And he picked up his hat and walked away.

It was almost dark when Gilly reached the third farm. As before, he asked for a job and, as before, he got it. The farmer's wife showed him to a tiny room with only a narrow bed and an old chest of drawers in it. Going to sleep, Gilly saw that the sheets and blankets were very old and were patched in many places. Nothing is wasted on this farm, thought Gilly.

The next morning, Gilly cleaned the stables
and brushed the horses.

He painted the wagon and weeded the
vegetables. That night he sat down to
dinner with the farmer's family.

Everybody helped themselves to fish but when the plate
was passed to Gilly, only the heads and tails were left. There
were only a few small potatoes swimming in a big bowl of water.

Gilly felt his temper rising. He was just about to open
his mouth, when he thought of his father's words: "Remember
the laughter that is in you."

Suddenly he stood up and ripped off his shirt.

The farmer's family was amazed. "Whatever are you doin',
young fella?" asked the farmer.

"Well," explained Gilly, "I just saw those two little
potatoes off there in the lake and I thought
I'd better swim for them!"

The farmer and his family laughed. They laughed so hard that they almost forgot about crumb time. At the end of every meal the entire family scraped every tiny crumb into a big dish.

When Gilly had asked what they were doing the farmer's wife explained, " 'Waste not, want not' is our motto here. Crumb time comes after every single meal we eat. Why, Gilly, you'd be surprised what a nice crumb loaf I can make at the end of the week."

She clapped her hands and the rest of the family started to scrape the crumbs into a dish. When they were finished and dinner was over, the farmer said, "Gilly, I want to see what kind of fisherman you are. We like to eat fish in this family, so tomorrow go to the river and do the best you can. Whatever you catch will be our dinner tomorrow night."

Gilly caught many fish. When he brought his heavy basket
home, everyone gathered around it. But as soon as he opened it
up the farmer's mouth dropped open. "What in the world have
you done with the middles?" he shouted.

"Oh," said Gilly, "I chopped them up and threw them away.
Since I have been here, I've never seen anything but the heads
and tails. I didn't know you ate the in-betweens too!"

For a minute the farmer looked very angry.

Then he began to laugh.

And then his wife and children began to laugh. When the
farmer finally stopped laughing, he said, "Gilly, you're quite a
lad! I always respect a person who knows the right way to
get what he wants."

Gilly had wanted more food and he got it.
For the rest of his life Gilly hardly ever lost
his temper. When things went wrong he
remembered the laughter that was in him.